How I met Bixie

Children's books series
Written and Illustrated by
Robert Knietinger

ISBN:978-1-946523-27-7

I'm sitting in my apartment watching TV again. it is so lonely here by myself. I wish that I could have a pet so I will go out now to find a pet to adopt. It will be so nice to have a pet to come home to. This apartment will not feel so empty. I would like to come home to a sweet little face, a pet I can cuddle up to.

I hope to find the right pet for me. I need to make the right decision to find the right pet. I'd better look at all my choices. Once I make my decision what kind of pet I want then I will be able to go shopping for toys for my new pet.

When I find a new pet I will make a decision on its new name. It will be hard to come up with a new name. This will make my life complete again after not having a pet around since when I was a kid.

I am going to the pet shelter to try to find a new pet. I am looking at a cute rabbit. I remember having rabbits in my backyard. I don't know if rabbits are friendly enough that you can play with them. They eat a lot then sleep. I don't think a rabbit is right for me.

So I am looking at some fish but I don't think that will work out for me. I had a fish aquarium when I was younger. It was fun but it was a lot of work feeding them and keeping the aquarium clean. The fish were fun to watch but you can't cuddle with them. I guess fish are just not right for me as a pet.

I walked around the pet store some more to see what I could find. I am looking at some lizards. They look pretty neat, like little dinosaurs. I wondered, do lizards eat bugs? I wondered if they are friendly. They seem pretty laid back just sitting under the hot lamp. They come from hot climates so need to be kept warm. Do I need to buy bugs every week to feed them to a pet lizard? Come to think of it, I don't think a lizard would be the right pet for me.

Then I came across some guinea pigs. The guinea pigs were so cute and they seemed so friendly. I knew someone that had guinea pigs when I was a kid, she liked having them. I learned a few things about taking care of guinea pigs after seeing my friend with them. You need to keep their cage clean, give them water and food regularly. They are too small though so I don't think that would be a good decision for me.

I looked around some more and was surprised to see pet tarantulas! They were kind of interesting. They looked content in their cage. You can't really play with them or cuddle either. I just don't think that it would be the right decision for me.

I asked the girl that works there what tarantulas eat and she went to find out for me. She came back and told me that they eat live beetles. The girl who works here said they really don't make the right pet for a lot of people, but some people love exotic pets. That's OK, I just want an ordinary pet.

I heard some birds chirping so I went to have a look. I found some parakeets. They seemed funny to look at. They looked like they were having a lot of fun singing together. They seemed very friendly so I asked the girl that works there to give me some information on them. She gave me all the information on them, where they come from, how old they get, what they eat and so on. I still don't think that they would be the right for me though.

The pet store also had some little hedgehog; they seemed like they were very laid-back.
I asked to learn more about them, turns out they are really lazy. They're not really lively so I don't think they would be the right pet for me. I did ask if I could hold one. That was fun because I could feel the spiky quills on its back. It was so small that it didn't hurt my hands. That was neat but I put it back knowing it was not the right pet for me.

I was so disappointed. I really want to get a good pet to keep me company at home. I came all the way to the pet store and am determined to find a good pet. I had fun learning about different animals and how to take care of them. I enjoyed looking at lizards, fish, birds and other animals but something wasn't right. I just could not find that special pet that I know would make great company for me in my new apartment. I finally gave up and decided it's time to go home.

She liked the food I bought for her. I loved its spirit but the ferret got out of its cage. I had to help the girl that worked there catch the ferret. It was very hard to catch them very fast. Once we caught it we had to put it back in its cage. I asked the girl to find out some information and see what ferrets eat. She came back and told me they eat ferret food and she said they make good pets why you need to watch them carefully so they don't get out. but they are not cuddly pets.

I looked at some frogs. They seemed really laid-back; they were just sit on some rocks in the aquarium. I asked the girl to get some information about them. She told me all the information on them and she told me they eat little bugs. She said they don't make good pets, you need to be a person that likes that kind pet. I don't think that would be the right decision for me to make.

The girl that works there said there are a lot of different pets, but you really need to make the right decision for yourself and your lifestyle. The staff asked me if there was anything else that they could help me with.

I've had dogs all my life growing up. I didn't want to have another dog, I wanted to get a smaller pet and try something different. Since I could not find a pet I liked, I asked them anyway, "Do you have dogs here?"

The store attendant said, "Yes, we have many kinds, all different ages." She took me over to the dog section. She just walked me through all the dogs that they had and let me look at each of them. I decided not to go with a dog because it would be too hard for my schedule. I work early and they would have to wait all day before I could take them out for a walk.

BLANKet

The girl that worked at the pet store saw I was frustrated. She asked, "Have you ever thought about having a ferret for a pet? They are really nice." I replied, "A ferret? I never knew you could have those as pets. May I see one?"

She led me to the part of the pet store where the ferrets were. They are long and skinny, they have a small head. They have special needs, they eat things like corn. Some are very playful and some just want to cuddle. They can make good pets because they like people, they also like to play with other ferrets.

They are a little more work than I was planning on doing. Cleaning their cages was not what I had in mind. I decided a ferret was not what I was looking for.

FeRRi+
woRLd

The attendant took me to another part of the shelter to show me something neat. It was a huge habitat for hamsters. It looked like a huge underground city, with plastic tubes going everywhere. It had some wheels that the hamsters could run on. They seemed very happy to live there.

I had one as a kid but not as big and colorful as this one. When I was a kid you had to take it apart and put the hamsters somewhere while you put new grass in because the old grass started to smell. It was a lot of work. I decided then that this is not the right pet for me.

She then asked me, "Would you be interested in looking at some ducks?" I say, "Yeah, that would be fun to look at." She took me over to the area to check them out and told me what kind of food they eat and how to take care of them.

It turns out, ducks are better for living on a farm. I just live in an apartment so it's not the best place for a duck. There are ducks that live in the pond outside my apartment though. In summer time they like to cool off in the creek together. They walk around to the other creeks nearby and like to nap together after they take a swim. One of my neighbors feeds them bread, they are always waiting for her.

I was frustrated and decided to leave. On my way out when suddenly, out of the corner of my eye, I saw a precious little cat. I turned around and went back to her. She reached out her paw from her cage and then I took her paw and looked at her sweet little face. I just fell for her. I told them this little cat is the right choice for me. Once this little cat reached out to me and I took its paw I knew we were right for each other.

I turned to the attendant and said, "So, if you could help me with the adoption, I would be very happy. Thank you. The staff took me over to look at some dogs. I told the staff that I had dogs all my life. I told them the names were Ruda maxi babe Chloe and I liked having all those dogs in my life. But I think the right decision for me in my apartment is to have a cat. It would be a lot easier to take care of.

I told the girl working at the animal shelter, "I found the one! I want to take this cat home!" She then had me fill out some paperwork. It turns out Bixie was a stray cat, they found her on the street. I found out that Bixie was five years old.

She had tooth decay so she had to have some teeth pulled. She also had some problems with her stomach and had surgery to fix that. I'm glad someone rescued her and now she can have a good home and spend the rest of her life happy with me. They gave me some cat food for free! I was really excited about that, they were so helpful.

The pet shelter had a supply store. I bought a bag of kitty litter and Bixie's litter box. There were lots of cat toys to choose from, there are little balls with bells in them, little fake mice and feathers on sticks. I picked up a few toys also.

The lady at the checkout counter looked at my new cat and said, "Congratulations! You are giving Bixie a good home. She is so sweet. You are a lucky guy to find her." I smiled and said, "Thank you so much, I will take good care of her."

Walking home, I thought to myself, "What a long day. I looked at so many animals. I finally found the right pet for me. Now my life is complete again I have a little friend to come home to after work. I know I will have my new little friend waiting for me at the door to greet me when I get home from work. Looks like you got a good one Robert."

So I am so happy that I adopted this little cat called Bixie. That name is so cute. I just love how sweet and friendly she is. I know that her and I will get along great. She is just the sweetest cat you would ever want to know.

I was so happy to take Bixie home with me. When we arrived, I took her out of the box so she could check out my new apartment to see how she liked it. Then I started to play with her. Once I set up her room she was very happy. She started eating some of her food that I poured in her bowl. I had something to eat also because I had a long day looking for the right pet.

She took right to my apartment, she did not seem afraid at all. She knew she had a new home. That made me feel good. She was five years old when I brought her home.

MAN CAVE

MY CAVE MY RULES

BiXies Room

CATS Lives

BiXies Home sweet Home

As the sun set, Bixie and I sat on the couch together. I turned on the TV and found a good movie. We started bonding, I pet her and enjoyed the sound of her purring. Looking back on the day, I thought it was a long, hard day trying to find the right pet. I found the right one for my lifestyle. I'll have Bixie for a lifetime.

The End

This book is dedicated to Jessica, Lisa, Katie
Kristina, Rebeca, and Cindy.

CPSIA information can be obtained
at www.ICGtesting.com
Printed in the USA
BVHW021346080521
606763BV00004B/467

9 781945 423277